Stories for Dementia Patients

STORIES FOR DEMENTIA PATIENTS

First edition. March 15, 2023.

Copyright © 2023 Liom Liom.

ISBN: 979-8215451052

Written by Liom Liom.

The mysterious letter

Mrs. Meier sat in her favorite armchair and contemplated the world around her. The flowers on the table were blooming magnificently and the birds were chirping happily in the garden. But despite all the beauty around her, she felt lonely and forgotten. Mrs. Meier had dementia and the memories of her life were like a book whose pages seemed to turn incessantly in all directions.

One day, however, she received a mysterious letter. The handwriting was strange to her and she could not recognize who the sender was. Full of curiosity, she opened the letter and read:

"Dear Mrs. Meier, I hope this letter brings a smile to your face. I am an old friend of yours and I wanted to show you with this letter that I am thinking of you and am still attached to you. I have many happy memories of our time together and I think you feel the same way. We went through so much together and I want you to know that I am still by your side today. Love, your old friend."

Mrs. Meier was confused, but also happy. She could not remember this friend, but the letter touched her deeply. It had been so long since she felt loved and wanted. She decided to keep the letter in her closet and take it out whenever she felt alone and lost.

In the coming weeks, Mrs. Meier received more letters from her mysterious friend. Each letter brought her joy and happiness and she no longer felt as alone as before. She began to recall some of her memories with this friend and smiled when she thought of their adventures together.

Then one day a last letter came from her mysterious boyfriend. He wrote that he was sick and that he would die soon.

But he promised her that their friendship would never die and that she would always remain in his heart. Mrs. Meier was sad and wept for her friend whom she had never really known. But she also knew that he would always be a part of her life and that she would cherish his letters and their shared memories.

And so Mrs. Meier sat in her favorite armchair and contemplated the world around her. The flowers on the table were blooming magnificently and the birds were chirping happily in the garden. But now she no longer felt lonely and forgotten, because she knew she had a friend who would always be by her side, even if he could no longer be with her physically.

The case of the stolen jewelry

Mrs. Schmidt was an elderly lady living in a nursing home. One day she noticed that her precious jewelry had been stolen. She could not remember when exactly it had happened and who could have done it. Mrs. Schmidt was very sad and upset. The jewelry had a special meaning for her, because it had been a gift from her late husband.

The police were informed and Mrs. Schmidt told them everything she could remember. But there were no clues to the thief and the jewelry remained missing. Mrs. Schmidt felt even more lost than before.

But then came the idea of organizing a search for clues. The residents of the nursing home were asked to remember everything they had seen in the last few days. Everyone could help, because there was always someone who had seen something. Together they looked in every corner of the home and asked everyone if they had seen anything. Mrs. Schmidt told her story and there were many who remembered how much the jewelry meant to her.

One day, as Mrs. Schmidt sat in her room, sadly lamenting the loss of her jewelry, there was a knock at her door. A young man entered and introduced himself as an employee of the home. He said he had found something and wanted to return it to her. Mrs. Schmidt could hardly believe it when he returned the jewelry to her. She was so happy and relieved that she hugged the young man and thanked him.

The young man explained that on his way home from work he had seen an elderly man holding the jewelry. He recognized him as a resident of the home and took the jewelry from him to return it. He had hidden it to protect it from further theft.

Mrs. Schmidt was so grateful for the help she had received from the residents of the nursing home and the young man. She realized that there were still people in her life who cared about her and were there for her. The case of the stolen jewelry had shown her that she was not alone and that she could always count on the support of others.

A mysterious inheritance

Mrs. Schmidt was an elderly lady who lived alone in a small house on the outskirts of town. One day she received a letter from a lawyer informing her that her cousin had died overseas and left her an inheritance. Mrs. Schmidt was surprised and curious, because she had not seen her cousin for years and did not know what to expect.

She made her way to the lawyer, who read her the contents of the will. Mrs. Schmidt could hardly believe it when she heard that her cousin had left her a villa in the south of France, along with a large sum of money. She was overwhelmed and could hardly believe it.

Mrs. Schmidt traveled to the south of France to accept the inheritance. When she entered the villa, she was overwhelmed by its beauty and elegance. But there were also mysteries to solve. For in a secret room in the villa she found an old suitcase with strange objects and a mysterious letter.

The letter said that her cousin had a secret and asked her to reveal it. Mrs. Schmidt was curious and began to investigate. She met people who had known her cousin and learned more and more about her life and past. Finally, she stumbled upon a secret that her cousin had kept for decades.

It turned out that her cousin had been a former spy who had worked for France during World War II. She had made her fortune from her adventures and her contacts with other secret agents. The suitcase and the items inside were evidence of her past as a spy.

Mrs. Schmidt was fascinated by her cousin's story and felt honored to be part of it. She decided to keep the villa and spend her golden years there. The inheritance had not only brought her wealth, but also opened an exciting new chapter in her life. She was happy and grateful for the unexpected turn in her life.

The mysterious burglary

Mrs. Müller was an elderly lady who lived alone in her house on the outskirts of town. One night she was awakened by noises and realized that someone had broken into her house. She immediately called the police and remained quiet while waiting for them to arrive.

When police arrived, they examined the scene and found that the burglar had entered through an open window on the first floor. Investigations revealed that the burglar had targeted her jewelry and other valuables.

Mrs. Müller was shocked and felt frightened. But she decided not to let it get her down. She began to do her own research and quickly realized that she had a talent for detective work. She interviewed neighbors and questioned people who had been seen near the crime scene.

In the process, she noticed that a suspicious car had been parked nearby on the night of the break-in. Ms. Müller decided to follow up on this tip and set off on her own in search of it. She found the car and took down the license plate number.

With the help of her research and the clue of the license plate number, she was able to provide the police with important information that eventually led to the capture of the burglar. Ms. Müller was proud that she was able to help solve the case and felt as if she had made a contribution to society.

The community honored her for her efforts and bravery. Mrs. Müller became a local celebrity and there were articles about her in the newspaper. She felt appreciated and fortunate that she was able to make a positive difference despite her age and loneliness. The mysterious burglary had changed her life in many ways and showed her that she could still play an important role in society.

The disappeared painting

Mr. Schmidt was an elderly gentleman who had been an avid art lover all his life. He had an impressive collection of paintings and sculptures that he had collected over the years.

One day he noticed that one of his favorite paintings, a picture by the famous artist Rembrandt, had disappeared. He had admired it a few weeks ago when he had gone through his collection. But now it was simply no longer there.

Mr. Schmidt was upset and felt helpless. He could not imagine who could have stolen the painting. He had installed an alarm system and constantly improved his security measures to protect his valuable works of art.

But then he remembered a young man who had visited his house a few weeks ago to organize a fundraiser. The man had claimed that he worked for a local charity and was collecting money for a good cause. Mr. Schmidt had been happy to help him and had even given him a tour of his collection.

When Mr. Schmidt remembered the man, he began to suspect that he might have had something to do with the theft. He decided to do his own research and remembered that the young man had left him a business card.

He called the number given on the business card and pretended to be interested in art. The young man did not recognize him and willingly gave him his address. Mr. Schmidt decided to go undercover and see if he could find any clues about his stolen painting.

When he entered the young man's house, he saw that there were many works of art on display. Among them was the missing Rembrandt painting. Mr. Schmidt was relieved and outraged at the same time. He immediately called the police and made sure that the painting was seized and the young man was arrested.

Mr. Schmidt was happy and relieved to have his stolen work of art back. And he was proud that he had solved his own case. The theft had shown him that he still had the talent, even at his age, to use his skills as a detective.

The kidnapped dog

Mrs. Meier was an elderly lady who had a faithful companion - her dog Bobby. Bobby was a small terrier who accompanied Mrs. Meier everywhere and always made her laugh with his cheerful nature.

One day, while Mrs. Meier was walking Bobby, the dog was suddenly kidnapped by a group of teenagers. The youngsters grabbed Bobby and ran away, leaving Mrs. Meier helpless.

Mrs. Meier was devastated. Bobby was not only her faithful companion, but also her best friend. She could not imagine how she would live without him.

But then she decided she wasn't going to give up Bobby. She called the police and filed a missing person report. She passed out flyers in the neighborhood asking everyone to be on the lookout for Bobby. She was determined to get her dog back.

After a few days, Mrs. Meier got a call from an animal shelter. They were informed that they had found a dog that looked very much like Bobby. Mrs. Meier immediately rushed to the shelter and found Bobby again. The dog had a few scratches and was a little scared, but he was otherwise in good shape.

Mrs. Meier was overjoyed to see her beloved dog again. She hugged him and kissed him and Bobby gave her a happy wag with his tail. She thanked everyone who had helped her find Bobby and decided never to let him out of her sight again.

Mrs. Meier was relieved to have Bobby back. She had proven that when you miss someone you love, you should never give up. Bobby and she were inseparable and happier than ever.

The haunting of the old house

In a small village there was an old abandoned house. It was said that it was haunted and no one dared to approach the building. But one day two friends decided to take up the challenge and explore the house.

The two friends, Tom and Lisa, were brave and curious. They were determined to find out if the house was really inhabited by ghosts. They packed their bags and went to the old house.

When they entered the building, they felt an eerie silence. It was dark and dusty and it smelled of decay. The two friends slowly walked through the house and discovered many mysterious things. Suddenly they heard a loud noise and the creaking of wood. They were frightened and were sure that they were being haunted by a ghost.

But when they turned around, they saw only an old man who turned out to be the owner of the house. He told the two friends that he had inherited the house and did not want to sell it for sentimental reasons. He had done some renovations, but it was difficult to keep the house in good shape.

Tom and Lisa were relieved that there were no ghosts, only the kind old man. They offered to help him renovate the house and he gratefully accepted. They worked hard to bring the house back to a habitable condition.

When the house was finished being renovated, Tom and Lisa decided to throw a big housewarming party. They invited all the villagers and celebrated until late at night. The owner of the house was overjoyed and grateful for the help of the two friends.

The house was now a beautiful home again and no one believed it was haunted. Tom and Lisa were proud that they had breathed new life into the old house and that they had helped the owner to revive it.

The secret of the abandoned mine

Tom has always been fascinated by old mines. He could read for hours about the stories of gold seekers and treasure hunters who searched for their fortune in the mountains. When he heard that there was an abandoned mine nearby, he couldn't resist exploring it.

With his flashlight in hand and a backpack full of provisions, Tom set out. The mine was hidden deep in the mountains, and the way there was arduous. Tom climbed over rocks and waded through rivers until he finally reached the mine.

The mine was dark and creepy, but Tom was not deterred. He was determined to discover the secret of the mine. He searched the corridors and shafts and finally found an old map.

The map led to a hidden treasure that an old prospector had hidden in the mine many years ago. Tom could hardly believe his luck, he had found the clue he had been looking for.

He followed the map to a secret room deep in the mine, where he finally found the treasure. It was a box full of gold and jewels that shone and sparkled in the glow of his flashlight.

Tom was overjoyed that he had discovered the secret of the abandoned mine. He returned to the valley, bringing the treasure with him. Now he could finally fulfill his dream and spend a lifetime traveling and discovering the world.

For dementia patients and seniors, this story is an exciting journey to a bygone era. It reminds them of the adventures of their youth and brings their imagination to life.

A false game

In a quiet neighborhood lived Mrs. Schmidt, an elderly lady who got along well with her neighbors. One day, Mrs. Schmidt noticed that her granddaughter, Laura, looked very worried. She asked her what was wrong, and Laura told her that she had won money in an online quiz, but had to give her bank details to receive the money.

Ms. Schmidt knew that online scammers use such tricks to obtain personal information. Together, they checked Laura's bank account and discovered that the money had indeed disappeared. They reported the incident to the police, but there seemed to be no trace of the scammers.

A few days later, Laura called her grandmother again and told her that she had been contacted by a "security company" that would help her reclaim the lost money for a fee. Ms. Schmidt knew it was another scam and decided to take action herself.

She contacted an old friend who was a former police officer and now specialized in fraud cases. Together they researched and found out that the "security company" was a fake company run by a man who had already been convicted of fraud.

Ms. Schmidt and her friend informed the police about this and were eventually able to catch the scammer. Laura got her money back and was incredibly grateful for her grandmother's support.

The neighborhood was proud of Mrs. Schmidt and praised her for her bravery and courage in putting an end to the scammers. Mrs. Schmidt smiled and said that she was just doing what she had to do to protect her family. She felt happy and satisfied and knew that she was able to protect herself and her loved ones from evil.

A surprise party

Once Fritz had a birthday and his granddaughter Anna was not only his biggest surprise, but also his greatest gift. Since then, the two were inseparable and spent every free minute together. When Fritz was about to celebrate his 90th birthday, Anna was determined to give him a very special surprise. She decided to organize a surprise party and invited all of Fritz's friends and family.

The preparations took several weeks and Anna invested all her time and energy in the planning. She knew that Fritz would not be easy to surprise, but she was sure that he would be very happy. On the day of the party, Fritz was in a particularly good mood and had no idea of the planned celebration. When he opened the door, all his loved ones were standing in front of him singing him a birthday serenade. Fritz couldn't believe it and tears of emotion ran down his face.

The party was a complete success and Fritz was overwhelmed by the love and care everyone showed him. Anna was overjoyed that everything had gone so well and she felt that she had given her grandpa an unforgettable gift. Fritz was full of joy and happiness, and when the party was over, he thanked everyone for this wonderful day. It was a day he would never forget and he was infinitely grateful for Anna and all the people who gave him so much love and joy.

A trip to the countryside

Anna and her friends, Maria and Peter, had not gone out together for a long time. They decided to spend a day in nature and took a trip to the countryside. They packed provisions and drove to the nearby national park. There they walked through forests and meadows and enjoyed the fresh air and the idyllic landscape.

They discovered a picturesque lake and sat down on the shore. They talked about old times and laughed a lot. Then they decided to have a picnic. They spread out a blanket and enjoyed delicious sandwiches and fruit salad. Peter even had a bottle of wine with him, which they drank together.

After dinner, they went for a walk until they finally got tired. They drove back to town, happy and satisfied with their day in nature. On the way home, they decided that they should do it again soon, since it was such a nice time.

The trip to the countryside had shown Anna, Maria and Peter how important it is to spend time together and enjoy the little pleasures of life. It was a day full of joy, happiness and unforgettable memories.

A journey into the past

Carla sat on her bed and stared into the air. She had the feeling that she was trapped in a dream. She looked out the window and noticed that there was a world outside that she no longer recognized. She couldn't remember the last time she had left the house. She had been home for years, since her husband had passed away. She felt lonely and forgotten until one day a letter sent her back in time.

Carla opened the letter and read slowly. It had been written by her granddaughter who lived in town. She had invited her to visit for a weekend. Carla was excited and scared at the same time. She hadn't visited the city in a long time and didn't know what to expect. But she decided to overcome her fear and accept her granddaughter's offer.

She traveled to the city by train and was met at the station by her granddaughter. They drove through the streets of the city and Carla recognized many places she had been as a young woman. They drove to an old mansion that Carla had visited many times as a child. It was now a museum and she was looking forward to visiting it.

At the museum, a young man showed her around, explaining how the mansion had been restored and how it was now used as a museum. As they walked through the mansion, Carla reminisced about her past. She told her granddaughter about her experiences and adventures as a young woman. She talked about her friends, her family and her husband. She laughed and cried as she shared her memories.

At the end of the day, they returned to their granddaughter's house. They had organized a surprise party for Carla. Her granddaughter had invited friends and family members that Carla had not seen in years. She was delighted with the surprise and overwhelmed by all the love and joy that was shown to her.

That night, Carla lay in her bed and thought back to that day. She had felt forgotten for so long, but today she felt like she had lived again. She thought of her granddaughter and how grateful she was for helping her return to the past. She knew that she would never forget what had happened that day and that it would always be a part of her past.

A day at the beach

The sun was shining in the cloudless sky when Marie and her grandchildren reached the beach. The soft sand tickled their feet as they sat down on a blanket and enjoyed the view of the sparkling sea.

Marie took a deep breath and felt the salty air in her lungs. She was grateful that she could spend this day with her loved ones. For she knew that life was fleeting and one should make the most of every moment.

The grandchildren were full of energy and ran to the water to splash in it. Marie watched them smiling as she suddenly remembered a previous day at the beach.

It had been many years ago, when she was still young and carefree. Together with her husband, she had taken a trip to the coast and enjoyed the day by the sea. It had been a day full of joy and happiness that she remembered fondly.

When she returned from her thoughts, she saw her grandchildren building a sand castle. She decided to help them and together they built a castle that was the pride of the beach.

As the day slowly came to an end and the sun set, they said goodbye to the beach. Marie felt fulfilled and happy that she could spend this day with her grandchildren. She knew that she would carry these memories in her heart forever.

A garden party

The sun was shining in the blue sky and it was a perfect day for a garden party. Martha had been waiting for this day for a long time and now it was finally time. She had invited friends and family and everyone had brought something to eat or drink.

The party was in full swing when Martha suddenly noticed that her favorite jewelry was missing. She had been wearing it that morning, but now it was gone. She was sure that she had brought it into the house, but where it was now, she did not know.

The guests tried to calm Martha down and promised to help her find the jewelry again. They searched the house and the garden, but without success. Martha was sad and disappointed, because the jewelry was of great importance to her.

Suddenly Martha heard a noise from the shed in the garden. She went over and opened the door. There sat her grandson Max, grinning cheekily at her. He had taken the jewelry and wanted to play a trick on Martha. But when he saw her face, he knew he had gone too far.

Martha was happy when she had the jewelry back in her hands. She was grateful for her family and friends who had helped her retrieve it. The party went on and everyone had a great time. Martha knew that this day would be memorable, not because of the lost jewelry, but because of the joy and happiness she had shared with her loved ones.

A visit to the zoo

It was a sunny day and the birds were chirping happily as the senior group entered the zoo. The air was filled with an excited buzz as they began to observe the various animals. There were lions, tigers, elephants, and even monkeys that made them laugh as they frolicked and got up to mischief.

The group sat down on a bench to rest when suddenly a little boy came up to them with tears in his eyes. "I lost my teddy bear," he sobbed. "I've looked everywhere for him, but I can't find him."

The group was moved and decided to help the boy. They split up and started searching the whole zoo. They also asked other visitors and staff about the teddy bear.

After a while they heard a loud squeak and followed the sound. It led them to a cage with some young monkeys who were having fun with the teddy bear. The boy was overjoyed to find his beloved teddy bear again and the group was happy to have helped him.

They spent the rest of the day looking at the different animals and talking about their adventures. The sun slowly set as they left the zoo, exhausted but happy and filled with wonderful memories. The day at the zoo was a great success and the group looked forward to the next adventure that awaited them.

A day on the farm

Mrs. Meier has been looking forward to her trip to the farm for days. She remembers her childhood, when she often visited her uncle's farm with her father. The fresh air, the animals and country life have always brought her joy.

When the bus finally arrives at the farm, Mrs. Meier is excited and happy. The farmer greets the guests warmly and leads them to the stables. Mrs. Meier pets the sheep and goats, and laughs when she sees the chickens running around her legs. She can still remember exactly the names of the animals she met on her uncle's farm many years ago.

The group also gets a tour of the fields where the farmer grows his various vegetables and fruits. Mrs. Meier is impressed by the variety and beauty of the plants. She remembers picking tomatoes in her grandmother's garden as a child and is pleased that today she has the opportunity to buy fresh vegetables directly from the farm.

After a delicious lunch with fresh ingredients from the farm, the guests set off on a carriage ride through the surrounding fields and meadows. Mrs. Meier enjoys the ride and the smell of hay and grass.

When the excursion comes to an end and Mrs. Meier is back at the retirement home, she is exhausted but happy. She thinks of the beautiful memories of her childhood and the wonderful day on the farm. She is grateful for the experience and looks forward to coming back soon.

A picnic in the park

It was a sunny day in spring when a group of seniors headed to the city park for a picnic. Everyone had brought something to eat and drink and they were all looking forward to spending some quality time together.

The group had found a nice spot under a large tree that provided pleasant shade. The picnic blankets were spread out, the food was unpacked and soon it was a merry circle laughing and chatting together.

Suddenly they noticed that a little girl was sitting alone on a bench, crying and holding her stomach. The group of seniors immediately rushed to the girl and asked what had happened. The girl replied that she had lost her purse and now could not get home. Immediately, the seniors offered their help to take the girl home.

On their way to the girl's house, the seniors noticed a group of children swimming in a nearby pond, even though bathing was prohibited there. As they approached, they heard an elderly man loudly asking the children to leave the pond. But the children ignored him and continued swimming.

The seniors realized that the man was the owner of the park and told him that they were willing to watch the children so that he would not have to leave them alone. The man was relieved and grateful for their help.

Finally, they arrived at the little girl's house. They helped her find her lost purse and brought her home safely. The girl's mother was relieved and grateful for the seniors' help.

The group finally returned to the picnic area where they were awaited by the children who had recovered from their swimming trip. They had prepared a small gift for the seniors to thank them for their help.

It was a wonderful day at the park where the seniors not only had a cozy picnic, but also had a chance to help others and make friends.

A cup of tea with friends

In a quiet, tranquil neighborhood lived Mrs. Schmidt, a loving, elderly lady. She was known for her hospitality and her friendship with many neighbors in her neighborhood. One sunny day, Mrs. Schmidt decided to invite her friends for a cup of tea and a nice chat in her cozy garden.

She prepared everything carefully and was excited to receive her friends. But when her friends arrived, Mrs. Schmidt noticed that her favorite cup, which she usually used on special occasions, was missing. She remembered seeing it in her kitchen before she had left to prepare the invitations. She searched the entire kitchen but could not find the cup anywhere. Desperately, she thought about how to serve tea to her friends when she suddenly noticed that one of the cups she had placed on the table looked a little different.

She turned the cup over and discovered a small piece of paper underneath, which she pulled out and read. On it was written, "I took your cup, but don't worry, I'll bring it back." Mrs. Schmidt was a little confused, but she decided not to think much about it and instead enjoy the tea party.

As the friends enjoyed the delicious pastries and tea, they noticed a mysterious figure appearing at the end of the garden. It was a young man who held the missing cup in his hand and returned it to Mrs. Schmidt. He explained that it was he who had taken it because he was so fascinated by the beauty and elegance of the cup. He apologized for the disturbing behavior and asked for forgiveness.

Mrs. Schmidt was touched by his honesty and sincere apology. She smiled and said, "I gladly forgive you, young man. You have given me a story to tell that I will never forget." The friends agreed with her and the young man was relieved that all was well.

It was a wonderful day celebrating friendship and forgiveness, and Mrs. Schmidt was grateful that she could be a part of it. She was sure she would have many more such days and looked forward to sharing them with her friends.

A joint handicraft lesson

It was a rainy day at the nursing home, and the residents had retired to the common room. Most of them sat quietly, reading books or solving puzzles, while others waited for their next meal. But that changed when Emma, a young volunteer, came in.

"Hey, everybody! Who wants to do something creative?" she called cheerfully.

Some of the residents looked up and smiled, while others remained skeptical. But Emma was not discouraged. She took out a large bag and spread its contents on the table: colorful sheets of paper, scissors, glue and other craft materials.

"I thought we could all make something nice together," Emma said.

The residents began to get involved and soon the room was filled with laughter and conversation. It was a day of reminiscing about past crafts and times with friends. One of the residents, Ms. Schmidt, talked about how she had sewn her own clothes as a child, while another resident, Mr. Braun, told stories about his adventures as an artist.

Then suddenly, when they were all busy with their craft project, Emma looked at her watch and exclaimed, "Oh no! We have to stop in a minute, I almost forgot I baked cookies for all of us."

The residents looked up and smiled, excited at the idea of getting cookies. Emma handed out the cookies and a cup of tea, and they all sat and talked until it was time for dinner.

It was a day they had all enjoyed, and they were grateful for the joy Emma had brought into their lives. Some of them might soon forget the craft session, but the friendship and sense of connection would remain for a long time.

A birthday full of surprises

It was a beautiful day in summer and Anna, an elderly lady, woke up with a smile. Today was her birthday and she was looking forward to spending the day with her friends. She had decided a few weeks ago to hold her birthday party in a nearby park where she could have a picnic with her friends and enjoy nature.

Anna got ready and drove to the park. When she arrived, the park was decorated with colorful balloons, garlands and tables covered with fresh fruit and delicious cake. Her friends had prepared everything perfectly to make the day an unforgettable experience.

They all sat together, talking and laughing and enjoying the delicacies. Suddenly, Anna heard a strange noise. She looked around and noticed a man looking around suspiciously. She was about to get up and see what was going on when her friends jumped up and revealed a huge surprise.

A big cake was brought in and on it were written all the names of her friends. The candles were lit and everyone sang "Happy Birthday". Anna could not believe how happy she felt at that moment. The fear of the unknown man was blown away.

The celebration continued and there were many more surprises. Anna received gifts she never expected and she was so grateful to have these wonderful people in her life.

At the end of the day, when Anna went home tired, she knew that this was the best birthday she ever had. She was surrounded by love, joy and happiness and knew that her friends would always be there for her.

The rescue of the little kitten

It was a beautiful day in summer when the residents of the nursing home got a little surprise. Suddenly they heard a loud meowing coming from outside. They went outside and saw a little kitten stuck in a tree calling for help.

The seniors decided to help the kitten and called the fire department. But it would be a while before the fire department arrived. In the meantime, the residents of the nursing home decided to help the kitten and a rescue plan was developed.

A group of seniors climbed the tree to rescue the kitten, while other residents secured the ground and took care of the animal's welfare. It was a difficult task, but they did not give up and finally managed to free the kitten.

When the fire department finally arrived, the kitten was already rescued and the seniors were praised from all sides. It was a proud moment for the residents of the retirement home and the kitten became their new pet from now on.

The residents spent the rest of the day with the kitten and had a lot of fun with him. They decided to give it a name and called it "Lucky" because it was really lucky to be rescued by the residents.

The rescue of the little kitten had brought the residents of the nursing home closer together and given them a sense of joy and happiness. It was a day they would never forget and it proved that even in old age great things can be achieved.

An encounter with an old friend

It was a sunny day in the park and Elsa, an elderly lady, was sitting on a bench watching people walk by. She remembered her youth when she often came here to play with her friends and enjoy nature.

Suddenly she noticed someone coming towards her. It was her old friend Martin, whom she had not seen for many years. She stood up, hugged him and they began to talk about old times.

Martin told her that he was in town to visit his grandson who lived nearby. Elsa was pleased that he was still in touch with his family and asked him to introduce her to his grandson.

The three spent the rest of the day together talking about their memories and having a wonderful time together. Elsa was happy that she had met her old friend again and that she was able to make a new friendship with his grandson.

When it was time to say goodbye, Martin gave Elsa a hug and said, "It was great to see you again, Elsa. Let's not wait so long to see each other again." Elsa nodded in agreement and Martin and his grandson left.

Elsa sat on the bench for a while longer, happy about the unexpected encounter and the new friends she had made. She knew that she now had something to look forward to the next time she came to the park.

A sunset at the lake

It was a warm summer evening as the group of seniors walked together along the lakeshore. They enjoyed the fresh air and the sound of the waves as they searched for the perfect spot for a sunset. One of the participants, Mr. Schmidt, talked about his younger years at the lake and how he often spent time here with his friends and family.

When they finally found a comfortable spot overlooking the lake, they sat down on the blankets provided and enjoyed the breathtaking view. The sky was bathed in warm shades of orange and pink as the sun slowly set. Everyone listened to the gentle lapping of the water and enjoyed the peaceful atmosphere.

But suddenly one of the seniors noticed that a small kitten was in distress on the opposite bank. It had become entangled in a piece of barbed wire and was unable to free itself. The group did not hesitate for long and decided to help the animal.

Together they went to the other side of the lake and found the little kitten in the middle of the barbed wire. They carefully freed it and lovingly cared for it. All were happy that they could help the animal and were happy about the new family member.

Back at the lakeshore, they sat together for a long time and enjoyed the beautiful sunset. Mr. Schmidt and the others shared their own experiences with pets and how much joy they can bring. It was an evening filled with joy, happiness and precious memories that would bond the group forever.

A musical soiree

It was a warm summer evening when the residents of the retirement home were looking forward to a special musical soirée. The organizers had prepared everything perfectly, from the decorations to the choice of music, to make the evening unforgettable. The residents gathered in the lounge, where they were welcomed by a trio of pianist, violinist and cellist.

The music began and the residents let themselves be enchanted by the sounds. Some hummed along softly, while others moved their hands rhythmically to the beat. The music reminded them of happy moments from their past. They told each other about their memories of musical events, dance evenings and concerts they had attended in their youth. The atmosphere was so pleasant and relaxing that some residents even fell into slumber.

After the break, a special guest was invited, a famous soprano who had come especially for the residents of the retirement home. She sang some opera arias with her clear and powerful voice, which captivated the residents. Some residents closed their eyes and listened attentively, while others quietly and devoutly sang along with the lyrics.

After the performance, the residents thanked us and clapped enthusiastically. They were overjoyed to have experienced such a special evening. Some spoke of how the music had revived them and refreshed their memories of times past. It was a wonderful evening and the residents were already looking forward to the next musical event.

A day full of laughter

It was a sunny day in the park and the birds were chirping happily. A group of seniors and dementia patients had arranged to have a picnic. The mood was relaxed and boisterous when suddenly someone started laughing. It was Elsa, an elderly lady with an infectious laugh.

The others joined her and soon the laughter sounded like a happy concert. The group told each other jokes and anecdotes and it seemed as if each joke became funnier the more often it was told.

Elsa began to tell a story from her youth when, as a young woman, she met a herd of cows on a mountain hike. The herd was very curious and followed her and her friends all the way. The group had so much fun with the animals that they decided to have a picnic with the herd.

The other seniors and dementia patients were enthralled by Elsa's story and began to share their own experiences. One told of a trip to the zoo with his grandchildren, another of a funny incident at the supermarket.

The mood was so cheerful that time flew by and the group decided to end the day with a song together. Everyone chose an instrument and they played and sang well-known songs together.

As the sun slowly set, the group said goodbye to each other and everyone went home happy and with a smile on their face. It was a day full of laughter and joy that they would remember for a long time.

A walk through the autumn forest

It was a beautiful day in autumn when Anna and her friend Marie decided to take a walk through the forest. The air was fresh and cool, and the trees were shining in the most beautiful colors. Anna and Marie put on their jackets and set off.

They followed the narrow path that wound between the trees, breathing in the fresh scent of autumn leaves and pine needles. It was so peaceful and quiet in the forest that they could hear the birds chirping.

As they walked along, they passed a stream that flowed through the forest. The water was clear and cold, and the leaves on the ground shone in the most beautiful autumn colors. Anna and Marie sat down on a bench on the bank of the stream and enjoyed the beauty of nature around them.

But suddenly they heard a noise from a distance. It sounded like a dog barking, but as they got closer, they realized it was a baby kitten. The kitten had gotten caught in a snare and was hanging upside down from a branch. Anna and Marie immediately ran to the kitten and freed it from its predicament.

The kitten was so grateful that it snuggled up to their feet and purred. Anna and Marie decided to take the kitten and give it a new home.

They continued their walk, enjoying the beauty of the autumn forest. The kitten followed them every step of the way and they decided to take it home with them after the walk.

When they got back to Anna's house, the kitten was happy and content. It had found a new home and a new family that loved it.

Anna and Marie decided to look at this day as a day full of happiness and joy. They had enjoyed the beauty of nature, rescued a little kitten and brought each other laughter and joy.

It was a day they would never forget, and they looked forward to sharing it with others and appreciating the beauty of nature and the joy of small things.

A delicious cake bakery

It was a sunny day in autumn and the air was full of fresh, cool air. A group of residents had gathered at the retirement home to bake a cake together. There was to be a colorful mixture of different cakes and pies and each resident was to make a contribution.

Eva, one of the residents, had been particularly looking forward to it. She had always been an avid baker and had a wide variety of recipes stored in her memory. She had decided to bake one of her favorite cakes, a moist carrot cake.

While the residents were busy gathering their ingredients and utensils, Eva was already in the middle of her work. She had put on her apron and was grating the carrots when her friend Lisa walked in. Lisa was a new member of the community and had only recently joined the nursing home. She hadn't been able to socialize much and was excited to participate in the cake baking.

"What are you doing?" asked Lisa, looking around.

"I'm baking my carrot cake," Eva said proudly, handing her a piece of carrot to try. "Do you like to help?"

Lisa nodded enthusiastically and Eva gave her a whisk. Together they stirred the batter and poured it into a cake pan. While the cake was baking in the oven, the two of them set about decorating it. They cut carrots out of marzipan and put them on the cake to give it that certain something.

When all the cakes were ready, residents gathered in the community room to show off their baking skills. There was a colorful mix of cakes and pies, from chocolate cake to apple pie to quark cakes. Residents sampled and enjoyed the various creations and shared recipes and stories.

Eva was proud of her carrot cake and earned a lot of praise from the other residents. She was happy to share her passion for baking and make new friends. The day ended with lots of laughter, good conversations and of course a delicious piece of cake.

A Christmas party with the family

It was just before Christmas and the family had decided to throw a big party to celebrate the holidays properly. Preparations were in full swing, baking, cooking and decorating. Everyone was looking forward to the upcoming celebration.

Grandma and Grandpa were also there. Although they were a bit older by now, they were still full of energy and joie de vivre. They helped where they could and contributed many great ideas. Grandma in particular had a knack for decorating and conjured up beautiful paper poinsettias and snowflakes.

On the day of the celebration, the mood was exuberant. The children romped through the house and everyone was looking forward to the upcoming feast. But before the time came, they sang together and told stories. Grandpa had a great idea and started playing his guitar. Quickly everyone joined in and there was singing together.

When the food was served, everyone was amazed. There was roast, potatoes, vegetables and as a crowning glory a huge Christmas tree cake. Grandma had baked it especially for the celebration and decorated it with much love.

When it got dark, the lights were extinguished and everyone gathered around the Christmas tree. The children had big eyes when the presents were distributed. But the adults were also happy about their gifts and exchanged happy glances.

The celebration lasted late into the night and everyone was happy and content. Grandma and Grandpa were overjoyed to be there for this special evening and enjoyed every moment to the fullest. It was a Christmas that everyone would remember. A celebration of love, joy and happiness.

A happy memory

It was a sunny day in spring when Emma sat on the park bench and reminisced. She had been alone for a while, enjoying the silence and the fresh air. Suddenly, she heard a familiar voice that pulled her out of her thoughts. It was her grandson Max, who had come to visit her. "Hello grandma, how are you?" he greeted her with a bright smile.

Emma was overjoyed to see him and told him about her memories of her youth. She told him about her first dance and her first kiss, about the friends she had lost over the years, but also about the friends who remained faithful to her until today.

Max listened attentively and remembered the many happy hours he had spent with his grandma. Then he had an idea. "Grandma, why don't we paint a picture together of one of those happy moments?" Emma loved the idea and together they went to Max's studio.

There they sat at an easel and began to paint. Emma painted a spring day when she and her late husband were happily walking hand in hand. Max painted a picture of himself and his grandma baking cakes together.

As they painted, more and more memories came up and they laughed and talked about the past years. After a few hours, the paintings were finished. They stood next to each other and admired their works.

Emma was so happy and grateful for this special day with her grandson. It was a day full of joy and happiness where they had created beautiful memories that they would carry in their hearts forever.

A treasure hunt in the garden

It was a sunny day in spring when Emma and her grandchildren decided to have a treasure hunt in the garden. Emma had prepared the treasure map in the morning and the children were excited to find out what they would find.

The treasure hunt began at the old oak tree in the garden, where the children found a clue that led them to a hidden key. The key opened an old chest that Emma had buried many years before. Inside the chest they found more clues and a treasure map that led them deeper into the garden.

They followed the clues through the garden, under bushes and across streams, and finally found the treasure hidden under a flower bed. The treasure consisted of small toy cars and sweets, but for the children it was an unforgettable experience to find the treasure.

Emma was happy that she could give such a day to her grandchildren. It was a happy memory that they would carry in their hearts forever. The family later enjoyed cake and tea together and told each other stories about past treasure hunts and adventures.

The day ended with happy faces and warm hearts, and Emma knew she would always remind her family of the importance of spending time together and making memories together.

An expedition into the animal kingdom

In a retirement home near a forest, the residents were avid animal lovers. One day, a group of them, led by Mrs. Müller, decided to go on an expedition into the animal kingdom. They had been observing wildlife in the wild for many years and thought it would be a great idea to share their experiences with the other residents of the home.

They carefully planned their route through the forest and got a map of the area. They also made sure they had enough food and drinks, since they would be out all day. They packed their binoculars, cameras and even some drawing materials to record their discoveries.

The group began their excursion early in the morning, and it wasn't long before they spotted the first animals. A group of squirrels were playing in the leaves and a herd of deer could be seen in the distance. The residents were excited and couldn't hide their excitement as they pulled out their cameras and binoculars to get a good look at everything.

As they wandered further into the forest, they passed a small stream where they could observe a water strider walking effortlessly on the surface of the water. A colorful woodpecker could be heard in a nearby tree. The group continued on their way and even spotted a fox scampering through the undergrowth.

They took a break and enjoyed their meals in a picturesque place. While doing so, they told stories and shared their observations. Some residents had the idea to draw the animals they had seen on their expedition. So they got out their sketch pads and drawing pens and started drawing the animals.

The group finally returned to the retirement home, happy and filled with new experiences and impressions. The expedition to the animal kingdom was a great success and all participants were full of joy about their discoveries. They were already planning the next expedition and were full of anticipation for what else they will discover.

A ride on the hot air balloon

Maria is an elderly lady who has always dreamed of flying in a hot air balloon. On her 75th birthday, her grandchildren decided to fulfill her wish and booked a balloon ride for her.

Maria was overjoyed and could hardly wait to make her dream come true. When the day of the balloon flight finally arrived, they met the pilot at the agreed meeting point. The pilot's name was Tim and he was a friendly man who had many years of experience in ballooning.

They got into the basket and the balloon slowly rose into the air. Maria was amazed by the beauty of the landscape and the feeling of freedom. She saw fields, forests and small villages that looked like toy models.

Tim explained to them the different controls of the balloon and how he controlled the speed and direction of the balloon.

He asked Maria if she would also like to take the wheel for once. Maria hesitated at first, but then she gathered all her courage and steered the balloon under Tim's guidance.

It was an unforgettable experience for Maria and her grandchildren. When they finally landed on solid ground again, they all laughed with joy and relief. Maria couldn't stop beaming and kept thanking her grandchildren and Tim for this wonderful day.

This day will always remain in their memories and bring a smile to their faces when they think back on it. It was an unforgettable ride on the hot air balloon and a dream come true for Maria.

A hike through the mountains

It was a sunny day in late summer and Marie, a spry senior citizen, spontaneously decided to go for a hike through the mountains. For a long time she had not felt the need to move in nature and breathe the fresh mountain air.

She packed a backpack with provisions and set out. It was a challenge for her, but she felt alive and full of drive. As she slowly climbed up the rocky path, she felt the soothing effect of the physical exertion on her soul.

She hiked for hours and enjoyed the view of the mountain landscape. Finally, she reached the top and was overwhelmed by the breathtaking view. She made herself comfortable on a rock and took out the lunch she had brought with her. As she ate, she reminisced about past hikes and felt grateful for the many beautiful experiences in her life.

As she was making her way back, she suddenly noticed a kitten that had lost its way and was stuck in a tree. Marie didn't hesitate for a second and climbed up the tree to rescue the kitten.

It was grateful and snuggled up to her as they continued their descent.

At the end of the day, Marie felt happy and satisfied. The hike had shown her that it's never too late to have new experiences and that even in old age you can still make a difference. She returned home with a big smile and the rescued kitten in her arms, ready for new adventures.

A boat trip on the river

It was a sunny day in late summer and the water of the river glistened in the warm sun. Emma and her friends were sitting on the bank looking out at the water. "I wish we could go on a boat ride," Emma said. "We haven't done that in a long time." The others agreed, so they decided to rent a boat and go down the river.

Emma and her friends were all seniors and some of them had difficulty getting around, but that didn't stop them from putting their plans into action. They carefully got into the boat and had a friendly young man push them off. They slowly cruised down the river, enjoying the fresh air and the picturesque scenery.

"How beautiful it is here," Emma said, looking out at the wooded shores. "It's like a trip down memory lane." The others agreed and began sharing memories from days gone by. They told of their own boat trips, of the journeys they had taken in their youth, and of the adventures they had shared together.

Time passed quickly and soon it was time to return to the shore. The young man helped them get out of the boat and they thanked him for the wonderful ride. "We should do this more often," Emma said, smiling. "It was such a nice experience." The others nodded in agreement and slowly walked back to their car.

As they drove back, they were still reminiscing about their boat ride together. They were all happy and content, and it felt like they had shared something wonderful together. It was an experience they would never forget and one that would bring them joy for a long time to come.

A voyage of discovery in nature

It was a sunny day in spring when Emma and her granddaughter Mia decided to go on a nature discovery trip. Emma loved spending time in nature and she was looking forward to sharing her love of nature with her granddaughter.

They packed a picnic and headed to a nearby forest. Emma had planned the hike well and she guided Mia along different paths so she could experience the diversity of nature. They admired flowers, shrubs and trees and watched birds and butterflies.

After a while they arrived at a stream and Emma showed Mia how to catch small fish with a landing net. Mia had so much fun doing this that she almost forgot that it was time for the picnic. They sat down on a blanket Emma had brought and enjoyed the view of nature while they ate their sandwiches and fruit.

After eating, they decided to continue walking and soon they came to a clearing with a small pond. There were many frogs here, and Emma showed Mia how to imitate their sounds. Mia laughed and tried too, until they were both sitting on the ground laughing from exhaustion.

When they finally left the forest and went back to the car, their faces were happy and their hearts full of joy. Emma knew that she had an unforgettable day with her granddaughter and that she could also teach her something about nature.

On the way home, Mia told her mother about the exciting day she had spent with her grandmother, and Emma smiled proudly. She knew that she had passed on her love of nature to the next generation and that she would always have a special bond with her granddaughter.

A ride on the historic railroad

It was a sunny day in the fall when the group of seniors and dementia patients got ready for a ride on the historic train. The anticipation of adventure was palpable in the air as they made their way to the train station.

The older gentlemen in their fancy suits and hats, and the ladies in their elegant dresses and hats, were reminiscent of another time. The younger attendants, who ensured the safety and comfort of the travelers, were also excited for the ride ahead.

When the historic steam locomotive finally arrived, the excitement grew immensely. The seniors and dementia patients were ushered into their seats and the steam locomotive began to slowly whistle and start moving.

The ride went through picturesque landscapes, past fields and forests. Passengers enjoyed the fresh air and the gentle motion of the train. Some told stories of previous train rides and other adventures, while others simply enjoyed the view and were lost in thought.

After a while, the train reached an old abandoned station. The attendants unloaded the passengers from the train and led them to a pavilion that had been prepared for them. Here there was a rich buffet with delicacies from bygone times. There were cupcakes, sandwiches, cheese, sausage, fruit and, of course, tea.

The passengers were delighted with the lovely design and delicious food. There was much to laugh and talk about as they enjoyed the moment and took in the surroundings.

Finally, the train returned and the passengers resumed their seats. During the return trip there was live music in the carriage, which invited to sing along and clap.

The ride ended at the station, but the memories of this unforgettable experience remained with the passengers for a long time. They talked for a long time about the beauty of the landscape, delicious food and cozy atmosphere on the historic train.

It was a trip that had left everyone in happiness and joy. The passengers were grateful for the opportunity to experience a bygone era in such a special way.

An expedition into space

The dementia patients and seniors had been looking forward to going to space for a long time. The expedition to space was the highlight of the year and everyone was excited as they got ready for the trip.

They were looked after by a friendly team of astronauts and scientists who made sure everyone was safe and happy. The passengers were dressed in spacesuits and given a short briefing before going into the spacecraft.

The expedition began with a gentle acceleration, while the passengers looked out the windows and the Earth became smaller and smaller. They could not believe that they were really traveling into space. The tension and excitement was palpable in the air.

After several hours, the spacecraft finally reached its destination - the moon. The passengers were amazed by the beauty of the moon. They got out of the spacecraft and began to explore the lunar surface. The astronauts explained to them the different craters and rocks and helped them move around on the surface.

The passengers were fascinated by the weightlessness and the feeling of freedom in space. They felt young and alive as never before. Some remembered the time when they were children and dreamed of traveling into space.

After some time, they returned to the spaceship and got ready for the return trip to Earth. During the trip, there was a celebration with food and music. The passengers danced and sang and enjoyed the company of the astronauts and scientists.

Finally, the spaceship landed safely on Earth and the passengers were greeted by their families and friends. They had had an incredible experience that they would never forget. The expedition into space had shown them that it is never too late to make dreams come true and that age is no barrier to adventure and discovery.

The dementia patients and seniors were grateful for the opportunity to explore space and make new friends. They had experienced happiness and joy and felt like children again. It was an unforgettable experience that would stay with them for a long time.

A journey through time

It was a sunny day at the retirement home when the dementia patients and seniors embarked on a journey through time. They had been preparing for this day for weeks and were full of anticipation for the adventure that awaited them.

The journey began in an old classroom that seemed to have fallen out of time. The walls were decorated with slates and pictures from decades past. The passengers sat down at the old school desks and imagined they were students again.

Suddenly it went dark and the walls began to glow. A bright flash flashed through the room and the passengers were transported back in time. They suddenly found themselves in another time - the time of their childhood and youth.

They roamed the streets of an old city and saw familiar faces they hadn't seen in years. They experienced anew the fashion, music and culture of their youth.

They visited old movie theaters and dance halls and felt young and alive again. They reminisced about times gone by and shared their stories with the other passengers.

They traveled through the decades and saw the world change around them. They saw how technology and science evolved and how society changed.

When the trip ended and they returned to the retirement home, they were full of joy and gratitude. They felt they had traveled back in time and were happy to share the experience.

They had created a memory that would stay with them for a lifetime. A memory of when they were young and the world was still ahead of them. A memory that showed them that life is full of adventure and discovery, no matter how old you are.

A day at the amusement park

It was a sunny day at the amusement park and the dementia patients and seniors were excited as they walked through the front gate. The smell of roasted almonds and popcorn was in the air and the sounds of children laughing and screaming filled the park.

The group started their day with a ride on the Ferris wheel, which lifted them up into the air and gave them a breathtaking view of the park and the surrounding area. The passengers laughed and joked with each other, enjoying the fresh air and the thrill of the ride.

Next, they went to the carousels and roller coasters, where they felt like children and overcame their fears. Some of them even tried the fastest and highest roller coaster in the park and were proud to have overcome their limits.

They also enjoyed the quieter attractions, such as the boat ride and the giant maze, where they put their senses and memory to the test.

Lunch break was taken in one of the park restaurants, where they fortified themselves with delicious French fries and hamburgers. While doing so, they told each other stories from their lives and shared their memories of past adventures.

In the afternoon they enjoyed the live shows and street performers that populated the park. They listened to music and danced with each other, enjoying the freedom and lightheartedness of the day.

As the day drew to a close and the park slowly emptied, they made their way back to the entrance. They were tired, but happy and satisfied with the day they had spent together.

They remembered that life is not over just because you get older. They had shown that you can still have fun and adventure at an advanced age.

As they sat on the bus back to the retirement home, they were already looking forward to their next outing and planning what adventures they would have next.

A surprise for Valentine's Day

It was the day before Valentine's Day and the residents of the nursing home were looking forward to the upcoming celebration of love. The staff of the home had decided to give them a special surprise and had planned a small celebration.

On the morning of Valentine's Day, there was a knock at the residents' doors and they were picked up by the staff in their nicest clothes and taken to the common room. There a surprise was waiting for them: a band played romantic music and there were tables full of delicious chocolate, cookies and cakes.

The residents were invited to sit down and enjoy while the staff offered them a glass of champagne. Some of the seniors were skeptical, but eventually they agreed and toasted to love with their glasses.

After they had eaten and drunk enough, the staff began to distribute gifts. Each resident received a card with a personal message and a small gift. Some received flowers, others jewelry or a box of chocolates.

Next up was a surprise: a visit from a local elementary school whose students had made Valentine's Day cards for the residents. The children handed out the cards and sang a song they had rehearsed especially for the day. The residents beamed with joy and some even started to cry.

After the performance, the residents and staff had a meal together, sitting and laughing. They exchanged stories and shared their memories of past Valentine's Days.

As the evening drew to a close and the residents were taken back to their rooms, they were grateful for this special day. They felt loved and appreciated and knew that even in their old age they were still special.

The staff of the retirement home felt happy and fulfilled that they could give this day to their residents. They knew that it was the little things that could bring joy to people and that love knows no age limit.

A picnic for two

It was a beautiful sunny day and the residents of the retirement home were outside in the garden. They were playing cards, taking walks or just sitting in the sun. A group of staff had decided to organize something special for two residents who got along particularly well: Martha and Klaus.

Martha and Klaus had met a few months ago and since then had developed a close friendship. They shared many interests and spent a lot of time together. The staff had decided to give them a special surprise: A picnic for two.

They prepared everything and invited Martha and Klaus to have a picnic together in the afternoon. They were led to the garden where a beautiful picnic set on a blanket was waiting for them. There were sandwiches, fruit, cake and tea, all lovingly prepared and nicely arranged.

Martha and Klaus sat together and enjoyed the food and the beautiful atmosphere. They talked about their favorite topics and exchanged stories. The sun shone warmly on their faces and they felt like in a dream.

When the picnic was over, the staff brought them back to the house and told them they had one more surprise for them. They led them to a room decorated with balloons and garlands. There, a small concert awaited them with a guitarist and a singer playing their favorite songs.

Martha and Klaus were happy and touched by the attention they received. They felt young and free as in their younger years. They sang and danced and forgot for a moment all their worries and problems.

As the evening drew to a close, they were taken back to their rooms by the staff. They fell asleep with smiles on their faces and the knowledge that they had a special friendship and beautiful memories that would bind them together forever.

A walk in the evening

It was a beautiful evening in spring, the sun had just set and the sky was slowly turning red and orange. A group of residents of the nursing home and their caregiver set out for a walk through the nearby park. The air was fresh and it smelled of freshly cut grass and flowers.

The residents were excited and looking forward to spending the evening together. They walked slowly, enjoying the scenery and pausing to listen to the sounds of nature. The caregiver told stories and explained the different plants and trees they passed along the way.

They arrived at a small lake and sat down on a bench on the shore. They watched the ducks and swans and listened to the birds singing. It was a peaceful moment that enchanted everyone.

The caregiver also had something special planned: She had a small bag with her, filled with snacks and drinks. She distributed the goodies to the residents and they started talking and laughing. The caregiver also introduced some games and puzzles that they could solve together.

The group continued their walk and finally arrived at a place where a little surprise awaited them: a live concert of classical music played by some talented young musicians.

The residents settled down on the benches and listened to the music. Some hummed along, others closed their eyes and let the sounds wash over them. It was a magical moment that would remain unforgettable for all.

The evening walk finally ended when the sun had completely set and it was getting dark. The group returned to the retirement home, happy and grateful for this special evening. They knew that they would always remember this moment and that even at their age it was still possible to enjoy life and have wonderful experiences.

A trip to the city of love

It was a sunny day in spring when a group of residents of the retirement home had a special trip ahead of them: a trip to the city of love - Paris. The residents were excited and full of anticipation as they boarded the bus and set off.

Along the way, they were able to enjoy the scenery and the caregiver told stories about the places they passed. The residents chatted with each other and shared their memories of past trips and adventures.

Finally, the bus reached Paris and the group began their exploration of the city. The chaperone had planned a special route that included all the major sights of the city. First they visited the Eiffel Tower and the residents were amazed by the height and architecture of the tower.

Afterwards, they went on to the Louvre Museum, where the residents admired the famous Mona Lisa and were amazed by the other masterpieces of art. The supervisor had also prepared a little surprise: a private tour of the museum, where they learned more about the history of art and artists.

After the museum, the group visited Notre-Dame Cathedral and admired its Gothic architecture and history. They also visited the Arc de Triomphe and the Champs-Elysées, where they enjoyed the boutiques and cafes.

For lunch, the group took a break and enjoyed typical French dishes such as croissants, baguettes and cheese. The residents enjoyed the French cuisine and shared their experiences.

In the afternoon, the group took a boat on the Seine and enjoyed the view of the city from the water. They admired the various bridges and buildings that passed them by and listened to the counselor's stories about the history of the city.

The day in the City of Love ended with dinner at a typical Parisian bistro. The residents enjoyed the food and drank a good wine while sharing their experiences and adventures.

The group went back to the retirement home, tired but happy and grateful for this special day in Paris. They knew that they would always remember this day and that at their age they were still able to have wonderful experiences and adventures.

An engagement in the park

It was a sunny spring day in the park. The birds were chirping happily and the flowers were in full bloom. The perfect setting for an engagement.

Emma and Max had been a couple for years and had already had many adventures together. Today, Max had a special plan for the day: he was going to propose to Emma.

They walked hand in hand through the park until Max suddenly stopped. He took a deep breath and began to speak: "Emma, you are the best thing that has ever happened to me. You make me happier every day and I want to spend the rest of my life with you. Will you marry me?"

Emma was overwhelmed by the question and tears came to her eyes. She nodded and fell into Max's arms.

They had a blanket and a picnic basket with them and sat down under a tree in the park. They enjoyed the sun, the food and each other's company.

They spent the whole afternoon in the park, planning their future together. It was the perfect day and they knew they would be together forever.

As the sun set, they got up and walked home hand in hand, ready for their new chapter in life.

A wedding in the garden

It was a sunny day in summer and the garden was full of flowers in all colors of the rainbow. The trees provided shade and a light breeze was blowing through the air. A perfect day for an outdoor wedding.

Johanna and Peter had met at the age of 70 and had been inseparable ever since. Today was their big day and they were looking forward to their wedding in the garden.

The guests slowly arrived and there were many hugs and joyful faces. The bride and groom stood in front of an arch of flowers and waited for the ceremony to begin.

When the music started, Johanna and Peter slowly walked down the aisle. Johanna was wearing a white dress with a bouquet of colorful flowers and Peter had on a suit in the color of the sea.

The ceremony was short, but very emotional. Johanna and Peter exchanged their vows and gave each other the rings. There were many tears of joy and satisfaction among the guests who were happy to be able to accompany the two in this moment.

After the ceremony, there was a festive meal in the garden under a large tent canopy. The food was delicious and the guests talked about love and life. There was also a dance floor and everyone was ready to spend the evening with music and dancing.

The sun slowly began to set and the sky turned orange and pink. It was a perfect day for Johanna and Peter, who celebrated their love with friends and family in the garden.

As the celebration drew to a close, Johanna and Peter shared a kiss under the floral arch and walked hand in hand back to their home. It was an unforgettable day full of joy and love that they would carry in their hearts forever.

A love story from times gone by

It was a sunny afternoon when Emma set out for the antiquarian bookstore downtown. She had set out to find an old book that her grandmother had always loved and often told her about. Emma had never read it before, but she wanted to finally pick it up and dive into the story herself.

Arriving at the antiquarian bookstore, Emma searched the shelves and finally came across an old book titled "Love in Times Past". It had an unusual cover and had obviously been read many times. Emma carefully picked up the book and began to leaf through it. The pages were yellowed, but the smell of old paper and ink made her happy.

Emma bought the book and headed home. As she sat in her room, she began to read and was immediately drawn into the story. It was about a young woman named Alice who lived in the 19th century and fell in love with a young man named Edward who worked in her father's factory.

The story was full of intrigues and obstacles, but despite everything the couple fought for their love. They experienced many adventures together and finally, after many ups and downs, they were united.

Emma couldn't put the book down. She was so captivated by the story that she felt like Alice and Edward, laughing and crying with them. She knew it was a love story from times gone by, but she couldn't imagine there ever being a love as strong as this.

When Emma finished the book, she felt happy and fulfilled. She knew that this story would stay in her heart forever and that she would always remember the unconditional love of Alice and Edward. It was a story that would go on forever, even when the book was long closed.

A joint boat trip

It was a sunny day in summer when Anne and her husband Peter decided to take a boat trip together. They hadn't spent time alone together in a long time and were looking forward to a relaxing day on the water. They packed a picnic and headed for the lake.

When they reached the boat, Peter helped Anne in and they made themselves comfortable on the soft cushions. They took in the calm waters and enjoyed the view of the green landscape on the shore. They reminisced about all the adventures they had had together during their long marriage.

As they slowly made their way along the lake, they noticed a group of ducks swimming beside them. Peter started feeding them bread crumbs, and Anne laughed as the ducks pounced on the food. They enjoyed the peaceful feeling that nature was giving them.

As they neared the end of the lake, Anne noticed that the weather had changed. Dark clouds were gathering and a wind was beginning to pick up. Peter realized it was time to turn around and head back to shore.

But suddenly the boat got caught in a violent wave and Anne became restless. Peter calmed her down, however, explaining that they just had to stay calm in such situations. He carefully steered the boat through the waves and brought her safely back to shore.

When they left the boat, a load fell from their hearts. They felt how their bond with each other had been strengthened and how important it was to spend time together. They hugged each other and happily walked back to the car, ready for the next adventure that awaited them.

At the end of the day, Anne and Peter knew that they would always remember this boat trip. It was a day full of peace, beauty and above all, love.

A romantic train ride

It was a sunny day in spring when Anna and Max were on their way to the train station. They had decided to take a romantic train ride and enjoy the beauty of the countryside. Max had planned a special surprise for Anna, which he would only reveal on the train.

As the train slowly pulled into the station, Anna and Max boarded and found their reserved seats in the romantically decorated carriage. The train slowly started moving and Max began telling Anna how much he loved her and how much she meant to him. Anna was beaming with happiness and couldn't wait to find out what Max had planned for her.

As the train passed through the picturesque countryside, it suddenly stopped at a beautiful spot overlooking the lake. Max led Anna off the train and showed her a big surprise - a picnic on a blanket overlooking the lake, surrounded by beautiful flowers and beautiful nature. Anna was overwhelmed and couldn't help hugging Max and telling him how much she loved him.

They enjoyed the delicious food and enjoyed the silence and beauty of nature. The scent of fresh flowers and the sound of water filled their senses and they felt like they were in a dream. After they finished the picnic, they got back on the train and continued their journey.

As they drove, they enjoyed the scenery and told each other stories about their past. They reminisced about the times when they had met and how their love had grown over the years. When the train finally arrived at its destination, Anna and Max knew that this day was one of the best in their lives.

They were grateful for the memories and the love they could share with each other. Together they enjoyed the rest of the evening in a romantic atmosphere and knew that their love would last forever.

A joint concert

Lena has always been a big fan of classical music. When she read in the newspaper that there was going to be a concert in her town with her favorite orchestra, she knew she absolutely had to go. However, she had no one to attend the concert with. So she decided to place an ad in the newspaper to find someone who would go with her.

It was not long before she received a reply. A man named Karl had seen her ad and wrote her a letter. He was also a big fan of classical music and would like to attend the concert with Lena. The two arranged to meet on the evening of the concert.

When Lena and Karl arrived at the concert hall, they were both excited. The music started and they were carried away by the sounds. The two felt as if they were on a journey through time and through different cultures. It was an incredible experience that they would remember for a long time.

After the concert, Lena and Karl went to a nearby café. They talked about their favorite songs and discussed how the music had influenced them. Lena was so happy that she had met Karl and that they could share this experience together.

Over the next few weeks, they met more often and attended more concerts together. Lena felt that she had finally found someone who could share her love of classical music and with whom she could share her passion.

That evening, Lena had not only enjoyed the concert, but also the company of Karl. It was a wonderful evening that she always remembered fondly and that reminded her that it is never too late to make new friends and experience new adventures.

A mix-up in the supermarket

It was a sunny day in spring when Maria went to the supermarket to do some shopping. She loved shopping in this supermarket because it was so big and had everything you could imagine. But that day everything was going to be different than expected.

As Maria strolled through the aisles, she suddenly saw an elderly lady who looked like her sister Anna. Maria couldn't believe it - Anna had died a few years ago. Maria approached the woman and politely asked, "Excuse me, are you Anna by any chance?"

The elderly lady looked at her in confusion and replied, "No, my name is Martha." Mary apologized for the confusion and went on her way to continue her shopping.

But as Maria left the supermarket and put her purchases in the trunk of her car, she was approached by Martha. "Excuse me, I know I'm not Anna, but I think I could still help you," Martha said.

Maria was surprised, but also curious. "How could you help me?" she asked.

Martha smiled and explained, "I'm here to visit my grandchildren, but I got a little confused and lost in the supermarket. I need help finding my way back to my car."

Maria didn't hesitate for a second and offered to help. Together they made their way through the supermarket while Martha told Maria about her family and how much she loved spending time with them.

In the end they found Martha's car and said goodbye warmly. Maria was filled with joy and happiness at the encounter and the opportunity to help someone. She thought about how easy it is to make a mistake in everyday life and that there is always a chance to help a stranger and feel happiness yourself.

And so Maria went home with a smile on her face and a warm feeling in her heart that sometimes it's the little things in life that can fulfill us the most.

A prank among friends

It was a sunny day in the park and a group of old friends had arranged to have a picnic in the green. They hadn't seen each other in years and were all very excited to meet again. They were laughing and telling stories of the past when suddenly one of the friends, who was always known for his jokes, came up with an idea.

He suggested that they play a game: Each of them should draw a piece of paper with a name on it, and then they should find the person and play a trick on him. The other friends were skeptical at first, but eventually they all agreed.

One of the friends drew Peter's name and decided to play a prank on him by stealing his glasses and hiding them somewhere in the park. Another drew the name of Maria and decided to serve her a huge piece of cake filled with mustard.

The friends went on to complete their tasks, and at the end of the day they all met again at the picnic table. They laughed and told each other what they had done. When they realized that Peter was missing his glasses and Maria had a bitter taste in her mouth, they all burst out laughing.

The friends spent the rest of the day laughing and joking together, and in the end they decided that they should do something like this more often. Even though they were old, they felt like children and it was a feeling they hadn't experienced in a long time.

It was a beautiful day in the park, and the friends went home with happy memories and hearts full of joy.

A funny circus performance

It was a sunny day when the residents of the retirement home received a special announcement. A circus would be making a guest appearance in town and they were all invited to attend a performance. Most were excited about the idea, but there were some who were skeptical. They remembered the circus performances of their youth and feared that they would not be able to keep up.

However, when they entered the tent, they were welcomed by a colorful and lively atmosphere. The circus performers wowed the audience with their breathtaking acrobatics and juggling skills, while the clowns made the audience laugh. A group of seniors was even invited on stage to participate in a funny performance.

The seniors were particularly impressed by the dressage of the animals. A herd of elephants marched into the tent in a long line and impressed the spectators with their impressive size and intelligence. The dressage of the horses was also impressive, and some seniors even recognized breeds they had owned as young adults.

Overall, it was an unforgettable afternoon and the seniors raved about the fun circus performance for a long time. Some said it was the best entertainment they had seen in years. At the end of the day, everyone was satisfied and happy to share this experience with each other. The memory of this day would stay with them for a long time and they would talk about it many times.

An unexpected encounter

It was a sunny day in the park when Alma sat on a bench under a shady tree and took a break. She watched the people passing by and enjoyed the mild spring weather. Suddenly, she saw someone she hadn't seen in many years. It was her old school friend Max, who had taken a seat on a bench nearby.

Alma and Max had spent a lot of time together as children and had been inseparable, but after school they had lost track of each other. Alma could hardly believe that she had met him again. She stood up and walked over to him. Max recognized her immediately and they embraced warmly.

They decided to relive their old times and spent the rest of the day together in the park. They visited the old playgrounds where they had played as children and walked through the green spaces where they had picnics in the past.

During the course of the day, they told each other about their lives since their separation and how things had been going for them. Alma learned that Max worked as a photographer after graduation and still enjoyed taking pictures. He even had his camera with him and suggested taking some photos of her.

They walked to a small pond surrounded by flowering cherry trees, and Max asked Alma to stand in her favorite pose. He pressed the shutter button and she heard the soft click of the camera. A few minutes later, Max had developed the photo and showed it to Alma. It was a beautiful photo with Alma framed by the blossoming cherry trees in the background.

When the day ended and it was time to say goodbye, Alma and Max promised each other to meet again soon. They exchanged phone numbers and said goodbye. Alma went home feeling happy and fulfilled. She had had an unexpected encounter and rediscovered an old friend. Life could be quite beautiful sometimes, after all.

A funny anecdote from life

It was a sunny afternoon in the retirement home and the residents were sitting comfortably together in the garden, telling each other stories from their lives. Suddenly, Mrs. Meier spoke up, "Do you know what happened to me once?" The others looked at her expectantly and Mrs. Meier began to tell:

"It was many years ago, I was just newly married to my husband Franz. We were still living with his parents in the house and I was cooking in the kitchen. Suddenly I heard a loud rumbling coming from the living room. I quickly ran over and saw that my husband was lying on the sofa, snoring loudly. But there was something else: a bird was sitting on his head! I couldn't believe what I was seeing and had to laugh. I woke my husband up and he seemed just as surprised as I was. We then tried to coax the bird out of the window and luckily it worked."

The others in the garden laughed and shook their heads at the curious story. Mrs. Meier beamed with joy that she had made the others laugh and told a few more stories from her life. The community in the retirement home had a lot of fun that afternoon and the funny anecdotes were talked about for a long time.

Imprint

LIOM LIOM
AUF DER HÖH 13A
35447 REISKIRCHEN
CONTACT
E-MAIL: sl350sl@gmx.de

Don't miss out!

Visit the website below and you can sign up to receive emails whenever Liom Liom publishes a new book. There's no charge and no obligation.

https://books2read.com/r/B-A-AOUW-ZLRGC

BOOKS2READ

Connecting independent readers to independent writers.

Did you love *Stories for Dementia Patients*? Then you should read *Stories That Make you Happy*[1] by Liom Liom!

[2]

Experience the beauty of life now in this unique paperback and be enchanted by stories that touch the heart and make you happy. These inspiring short stories explore themes such as the power of thought, the joy of discovery, or the path to fulfillment - each one telling in its own way about the beauty in the here and now and the happiness that surrounds us. Let yourself be enchanted by these stories and find new perspectives that will enrich your life.

---

1. https://books2read.com/u/bxry2J

2. https://books2read.com/u/bxry2J